MW00805249

# The Only Magic Book You'll Never Need

By **D.K. Brantley**
Illustrated by **Ekaterina Khozatskaya**

If you're reading this, you've probably been referred to as an oddball, a unique critter, or a weirdo at some point. Because no one reads this section of a book. After all, this is where the boring stuff resides, information about the book's guts. And that's included below. But there's also a heartbreaking tale, full of intrigue, for readers like you. Since you've made it this far, steel yourself for my tale. I planned to present this book as it is: a helpful how-to for the developing magician. Unfortunately, my publisher, leery of legal action, requested—nay, demanded—the book be deemed fiction. This demand was made in order to avoid litigation should an unskilled phony attempt these tricks with negative results. After aggressive negotiation, I caved and allowed this masterpiece to be labeled as something it is not: humorous fiction. The powers-that-be also added a letter to the title, changing *The Only Magic Book You'll Ever Need* to *The Only Magic Book You'll Never Need*. I felt this was off-putting. They insisted the change was no big deal. I hope Sir Brody's spineless management team is happy. I am not.

Published by Sir Brody Books | Cleveland, Tennessee USA | sirbrody.com | @sirbrodybooks


ISBN 978-0-9978611-1-2 (paperback)

Printed (most likely) in the United States of America

Illustrations by Ekaterina Khozatskaya, instagram.com/betweenthebars_spb

Edited by Jessica Brantley and Roger Schmurr

Fact-checked in whole or in part by Lindsey Aquila, Grey Briggs, Kristy Hinson, Christyne Morrell, and Donny Seagraves

May this not paint a black mark upon any of the aforementioned individuals' careers.

This book is dedicated to the Magnificent

______________________________________,

*Your name here*

who is one illusion away from being recognized as the most important magician of

the ______________________ century.

*Century in which you exist*

May your autographed memorabilia bring top dollar at auction
and paparazzi chase you down every street upon which you walk.

# Table of Contents

# Introduction

When Dedi first performed the disappearing balls trick in 2600 BC, people were mesmerized. Impressed. Frightened. Overwhelmed. Overjoyed. Over.... Okay, you get the point. They liked it.

There was, unfortunately, a problem. Smarter audience members knew the disappearing balls and other tricks were just that—tricks. They realized that you could pull a rabbit out of a hat because you were good at hiding rabbits in your waistband. You made yourself levitate with the help of a hidden metal contraption. Or maybe you could palm a card so well that even you forgot it was there.

But what if there could be more to magic? What if you could do magic tricks—even old tricks that have been done time and again—in new ways that no one has seen and no one can explain? That's where this book comes in.

Before you get into the heart of this book, it's best you understand that the techniques offered for these common tricks aren't common. They require more effort than many are willing to exert and will force you to do things others aren't willing to do.

However, if you're willing to do what other magicians aren't, you're ready to go where few magicians have gone: immediate stardom. Master the techniques in this book and you'll skip the children's birthday scene, avoid the ridicule that young magicians necessarily suffer from their peers, and skyrocket straight to a permanent slot in Vegas.

Sound too good to be true? Oh, it is! But enough about that.

Now, on with the show!

# The Only Magic Book You'll Never Need

# Sawing Someone in Half

**Difficulty:** 19 out of 10
**Risk of Receiving Court Summons Afterward:** 8 out of 10

Yes, this is a large-scale, intimidating trick with which to start such a humble book. But the book must begin somewhere. And like the nice lady at the tattoo parlor said, "Go big or go home." (I understand that many of you may be far from home while reading this. If that's the case, relax. The phrase "Go big or go home" isn't a plea with you to go home if you're not willing to do something "big." It's just a way to make you feel like a pansy if you don't. We'll go big out of respect for the phrase—not for fear of going home.)

If you've watched enough magic shows, you probably have a decent idea how the modern performer pulls off this trick. As you, the educated magician-in-training, probably guessed, no one is actually getting sliced into multiple parts.

That all changes with the following ground-breaking, bone-crunching technique. But don't go cutting people up just yet. To make sure your trick ends with a once-severed torso being reunited with its lower half, you'll need the right tools and one very special assistant.

The setup is typical. An assistant* (this one doesn't need to be all that special) climbs into a rectangular box that is approximately the length of a normal person. Make the box short enough to allow the assistant's head and feet to hang comfortably out of either end. (Here the word *comfortably* doesn't mean your assistant will be comfortable. Your assistant won't be comfortable one bit. The word *comfortably* indicates that her feet and head easily extend beyond the box. Yes, I could have used a different word, but I like the word *comfortably* and used it before realizing it would require such an exhaustive explanation.)

After situating the assistant in the box, pull out a gigantic saw and cut your assistant in two. Should you like the job to be easier, precut the box into two pieces. This way, you only have to run the saw through the flesh and bone of your assistant without cutting through plywood at the same time. (Doing this will speed up the sawing process and reduce the risk of your assistant suffering splinters or infection.)

Before moving forward, a quick note about saws. You will want a stainless steel version, as certain fluids are likely to rust the saw over time. Also, while some magicians feel the need to ramp up the excitement by substituting the traditional handsaw with a chainsaw, avoid this. Using a chainsaw increases blood loss and makes it more difficult to complete the trick. Finally, before taking the stage, heat your saw. When the blade begins to glow red or white, give it a few moments to cool, and continue.

As you saw the body in half, be sure to cut above the hip bone. You need your assistant nimble and happy to continue serving by your side. Therefore, helping her avoid hip damage due to poor saw placement is essential. Additionally, hip replacement is expensive! Since you will likely be held financially responsible for the procedure, avoiding the hip altogether makes good fiscal sense.

Anyway, once you have sawn your assistant in half, pull the box apart. Unlike other methods of performing this trick, you won't want to leave the blade in the box. Doing this ruins the effect. Since you used a properly heated saw, the wound should be properly cauterized, diminishing blood loss. (Note: An improperly cauterized body quickly becomes a cadaver. That is not magic.) And thanks to the use of a stainless steel saw, keeping your instrument clean of infection-causing bacteria is a snap! (It may be hard to believe, but with the right blade heated to the right temperature, you won't need a single squirt of antibacterial soap to keep your saw free of germs.)

At this juncture, you may be wondering how this qualifies as a trick. After all, sawing someone in half is usually called homicide and is frowned upon by all but the basest elements of society. Well, future magic-maker, it's murder in this case also—if you stop here. But you don't stop here. Because you're not a murderer. You're a magician. True, both start with the letter *m*, but that's nearly all they have in common. (Parenthetical remark [hence the parentheses]: Don't undertake this trick until you read the entire methodology and [A] have at your disposal all necessary tools and assistants or [B] are a trained undertaker.)

Prior to attempting the trick, you will need to procure the services of an unusual

individual. Should you find such an individual, kiss your mama, because this person has been sought by magicians throughout the ages. The only magician rumored to have found one was Oliver Sherbaum, whose act in the 1700s left crowds amazed and a-puking. Who is this person who will take your act from certain death to death-defying? A tiny person. As in Thumbelina tiny. But don't be fooled! Simply finding someone who is no larger than a thimble won't make this trick work. You need someone this size who is a master of the surgical arts. And that is no easy task. Especially since the tiny race of people responsible for birthing tiny surgeons is almost never seen by humans.

Assuming you find a tiny surgeon, continue reading to learn how to use him to your magical advantage. Without this surgeon, don't even build the box in which your assistant (not the tiny surgeon assistant, but the other one) shall be cut in two.

Now that the only readers left have found a tiny surgeon, I will continue.

With a tiny surgeon at your service, you've earned the right to know the secret of this trick. Inside the box in which you slice your regular-sized assistant in two, build a hidden compartment in which your tiny assistant surgeon will hide. The only time your surgeon will come out from the compartment is when you push the two box parts back together.

Until then, wheel the separated body halves around the stage for all to see. The sight of a severed human may bring much of your audience to a state of shock, but that's what magic has always done to an unsuspecting crowd.

After displaying the body, there's little left for you to do, Mr. Non-Surgeon. If you were a small enough surgeon, you'd be inside the box, and your assistant, even if the size of Thumbelina, would be the magician. Since you're reading this book and not *The Only*

*Surgery Book You'll Ever Need* (likely to be published under a modified name by my panicky publisher), you obviously fancy yourself more magician than surgeon. So leave the surgery to the pro.

To let the surgeon begin his good work, push the two box halves together. Do note that surgically repairing a severed body is complicated. Therefore, give your little surgeon plenty of time to work. Here are a couple ways to buy time without your audience growing suspicious.

**1. Perform other tricks.** This a great way to add suspense to your act, as the audience wonders if you've forgotten about the body lying in a box on the stage. Use this time to perfect new tricks and don't be afraid to make mistakes. It's okay if you guess the wrong card. With a body nearby cooling to room temperature, no one will notice if you pull out an eight of hearts instead of the three of clubs.

**2. Tell some jokes.** If you prefer jokes to more illusions, you're in the wrong line of work. Regardless, should you opt for jokes, avoid dark humor, as your audience is already in a dark state of mind. Instead, crack lighthearted jokes to help the audience forget the decaying body on stage.

Assuming you recruited a skilled surgeon, you can eventually release your full-sized assistant from the box in which she was sawn in two. Just make sure your once-sawn assistant is presentable. To achieve this feat, your surgeon must have various cleaning agents immediately available. This will permit the surgeon to remove blood stains from the clothing of the victim.** Remember: a bloody mess diminishes the effect.

Once you show the audience that your assistant is back in one piece, help her off the stage. Backstage, offer her a cup of grape juice or sports drink to replenish fluids lost during the trick. A small bag of animal crackers may be helpful. As may an IV with fluids and antibiotics, pain medication, smelling salts, and a quick trip to the ER. This last step may be excessive, but tiny surgeon sutures often struggle to stay sutured when stress is placed upon them by regular-sized assistants.

A simple trick? No. One that will set you apart from the rest of those hacks? You can bet your life on it. Your regular-sized assistant certainly will.

**Because this trick is performed with a new method that doesn't require the help of someone who knows how to avoid getting cut in half, you can use a volunteer from the audience. But choose wisely. You don't want a weakling who may pass out.*

***This word was initially* assistant, *but my publisher claimed the word* victim *gives the illusion more pizazz. I pleaded with my publisher to use another word, insisting* victim *would cause undue scandal. However, since I am—like so many of my contemporaries—obliged to obey my publisher in order to make a living, I relented.*

# Headless Dove

**Difficulty:** 8 out of 10
**Likelihood of Having Your Tux Ruined by Dove Poo:** 2

I don't want to give away how certain magicians perform this trick, but it's less than impressive. In fact, were a toddler to hear the technique, the kid could perform it without much effort. That said, there are many ways to pull off the classic headless dove. (Pun intended.) The dove can be a homemade creation with its own special touches or for a generic effect, it can be bought from the purveyor at a magic shop. The problem is that anyone can use these methods and yield the expected results: a yawning crowd.

To make this trick lively, as originally intended, you'll need to travel to Cape York Peninsula, Australia. At this remote locale, an extraordinarily rare species of bird exists. Its habitat is so deep in difficult terrain that this animal doesn't fear human intervention or anything else. It is the headless dove. And apparently, because it has no head, it can't sense danger and therefore has no capacity to fear.

To find a dove that will remain headless its entire life, you must capture it the moment it hatches. Though the headless dove lives its entire life sans head, the parents of the headless dove are fully headed. According to biologists, the whole can't-see thing cramps the style of headless doves, so they never have offspring. How, then, does the headless dove come to exist?

Two white-headed doves (Columba leucomela* for the ornithologists in the crowd) produce a single headless dove when a clutch of thirteen eggs hatches. How do you know which egg will produce a headless dove? By finding the smallest egg in the batch.

But be careful. With the white-headed dove, all eggs are small to the untrained eye, and more than one egg may produce a dove that is initially headless. However, all chicks but that which comes from the smallest of thirteen eggs will eventually grow a head. And while it's neat to watch a dove develop a head before your eyes, if that happens in the midst of your act, it ruins the effect. Because suddenly you're stuck with a headed dove. And no one finds that interesting.

With your specially bred bird in hand, pop a fake head on top of the bird's neck. Of course, the artificial head doesn't have to be birdish. Toss on the head of a mangled doll or an unwanted action figure. Or if you're feeling sassy, use a custom bobblehead made in your likeness. Crowds will love it!

Attach the head with double-sided tape prior to showtime. On stage, present the bird to your audience, and then remove its head with dramatic flare. Since the head is fake, the bird feels only a tinge of pain from the tape pulling on its neck. From this point,

do as you please with the headless creature. Toss it in the air, stomp on its plastic head, or let the bird walk around aimlessly on stage as you perform other tricks. The dove itself is a marvel to behold, so your work is minimal.

One consideration: White-headed doves are only white on their heads. The rest of the body is the color of asphalt. Since your dove is headless, it won't have any white part. Because completely white doves are most visible on stage, you'll need to remedy this. For years, I attempted to force my headless dove into a white tuxedo. This was not an easy task, and once I got my aviary assistant in the tux, the bird constantly had ring around the collar. So I spray-painted the bird. Yes, it sounds inhumane. But a friend living in an extended-stay motel informed me that the only risk associated with spray paint is inhaling the fumes. Since the headless dove can't inhale, spray-painting the bird is completely safe.

Once the audience tires of the bird, stick its head back on, jam the bird in a cage, and have an assistant cart the cage out of the audience's view.

**Bird enthusiasts are likely scoffing, since the Columba leucomela is actually a pigeon and not a dove. Well, congratulations, bird snobs, you caught me! Now go find a headless dove that's not a pigeon, and you'll really impress me.*

# Make It Snow

**Difficulty:** 3 out of 10
**Memorable Scale:** 10 out of 10

This one may be easy to execute, but it can't be done by just anyone. It takes someone who's brave and stealthy. Someone like you. Yes, you, dear reader-magician-in-training! So puff out your magic chest with pride, because you're about to learn the ancient art of making snow on the sly.

It starts with a quick trip to the store—one of those places that sells stuff in bulk. You're going to need cotton balls. Lots of cotton balls. More cotton balls than fit in your cousin's pickup truck.

Cotton balls in tow, head to your audience's homestead. Aside: I'm using the term *audience* loosely. As you will see, there won't be anyone around to see the illusion taking

place. They'll only know of the trick after its completion. Most likely, they won't know who is responsible for the magic. But that's okay. Sometimes, magic is about wonder, and contrary to popular belief, you don't always have to get credit for your skills.

For the best results, go to your enemy's—er, audience member's—home after 11 p.m. This ensures maximum darkness and increases your likelihood of pulling off the prank without your methods being uncovered.

In the dark of night, scamper around, spreading cotton balls indiscriminately. To give the snow a more authentic look, place some cotton balls on window sills, car hoods, and across tree branches.

Since a powerful wind can blow away your hard work, consider how to keep the cotton balls in place. I prefer misting. This can be done prior to heading to your chosen locale, but can be a bit messy. A better choice is to use a water hose on site. But be careful! Your sleeping audience may awaken if the faucet makes a high-pitched whining sound. If this occurs, a confused audience member may shoot you. This will ruin the illusion and your entire evening. To make matters worse, you'll have some explaining to do when you wake to your mother crying by your hospital bedside.

To use the resident water faucet safely, access it during the day. Turn the water on slightly and escape undetected. If the homeowner comes out during the day and asks what you're doing, ad lib like the champion that you are.

Now back to the magic...

Spray down the cotton balls. Once the cotton is in place and properly misted, get out of there. The rest of the magic takes place in the audience's eyes, where true magic occurs. No, you won't be on site to enjoy their looks of glee, but rest assured that upon waking to a yard of glistening white snow, your audience members' mouths will drop open. They will scream, possibly from joy. In many cases, these screams will turn to murmurs of delight, as they work tirelessly to remove the snow from their property.

To maximize the illusion's effect, don't reveal yourself as the creator of the winter wonderland. This enhances the effect of the snow and preserves your life.

Note of Finality (so named because it is the last note for this particular, peculiar illusion): Gorgeous as this effect is, it's not always met with a positive response. In the southeast region of the United States of America, even the threat of snow causes a societal breakdown. Schools close, hospitals lock their doors, stores run out of milk and bread, and housewives leave sinks full of dishes. Should you dwell anyplace where snow is a foreign and feared substance, skip this trick, and stick with kinder illusions that won't ruin anyone's day.

# Disappearing Boat

**Difficulty:** 6 out of 10 (unless you lack carpentry skills or a submarine; then, it's impossible)
**Cuteness Scale:** Off the charts

If you're a fan of popular television, you may have chuckled at how master magician Gob Bluth made his family yacht disappear on the hit show *Arrested Development.* For those unfamiliar with the episode, Gob put a hole in the vessel and let it sink. It was effective, but rather expensive. Fortunately, there is a better way. Because a boat that sinks and forever stays in the middle of the lake, pond, river, ocean, sea, or bathtub is rendered useless, particularly for magical purposes.

Don't suppose you can do this on the cheap though. You'll need a bona fide submarine. And a big one. You're doing magic, and in magic, bigger is always better.

Unfortunately, I can't provide the exact blueprint on how to work this out. This book doesn't have that much space. Besides, giving blueprints would rob you of the character-building process of figuring it out on your own. That said (or typed), I can tell you the general idea behind it. You're building a yacht around your submarine, with a dinghy on top—a vessel known as a submayaghy.

You may wonder why you need to cap a submayacht off with a dinghy, turning it into a submayaghy. The answer is simple: for getaway purposes. In the unlikely event a crowd is watching, you'll need your submayaghy to escape the scene without raising eyebrows. Granted, you could put the entire thing underwater, but that doesn't have the same drama.

I can tell by your sigh that you don't believe me. Allow me to explain, Mr. Skeptic.

Let's assume you've built a submayaghy. Let's also assume that you promoted yourself well enough to have a group of people standing around to see your illusion.

Start by pointing to your submayaghy, which floats nearby like an average seaworthy vessel. (Call the submayaghy a boat or a yacht, not a submayaghy. This will reduce suspicion.) The crowd will ooh and aah. Enjoy this moment. Because if things go south, this is the only time you'll impress the crowd.

After explaining the difficulty of the illusion, use a curtain to block the audience's view. If you don't have a curtain large enough to cover the breadth of the submayaghy, make sure your audience is very small and very close to your undersized curtain.*

As soon as you close the curtain (or have the audience step closer to the curtain so they can't see around it), push a small button inside your tuxedo. This will send your submayaghy into submarine mode. Assuming you crafted the yacht portion of your sub-

mayaghy with materials that allow the structure to sink with ease, the submersion process should take no more than twelve seconds. Typically, it should take only ten seconds, but allow a bit longer for insurance.

With the boat submerged, push the button in your other sleeve to engage the submarine motor. Just as the curtain opens, your audience will see only a dinghy floating toward the sunset. For added effect, place a puppy and kitten in the dinghy with oars strapped to their paws. The crowd will go gaga for the cute little critters that appear to be rowing whilst on a romantic cruise.

One consideration. Before unveiling this trick, test and determine the depth at which you will submerge your submayaghy. Set it too deep, and your dinghy will take on water. This will excite the crowd in a negative way, particularly if cute animals are onboard. Let it go too shallow and this, too, will be disconcerting, as it will appear that a blue whale is about to breach and consequently capsize your fur-filled dinghy.

**In extreme circumstances, forget the curtain and ask your audience to close their eyes. Example of an extreme circumstance: You used all your money to build the submayaghy and have none left for a curtain. Should you resort to this method, implement a strict no-peeking policy.*

# Indian Rope Trick

**Difficulty:** 6 out of 10
**Risk of Suffering Indian Rope Burn:** 7 out of 10

Any magician worth her salt knows there are tons of rope tricks. You can cut ropes up and have them magically come back together (see page 83), use them to aid in other tricks, and even jump over swinging rope in a rhythmic manner. This last method is also known as jump-roping and is not considered a magic trick. For the uncoordinated, however, it's pretty close.

That said, there is one rope-centric trick that takes the cake: the Indian rope trick. For readers in the United States of America, the Indians in question aren't from your country. There are no Indians from America. Those are Native Americans, and if my understanding is correct, they're tired of being labeled inappropriately. Anyway, this trick

has more pizzazz than any other rope-affiliated trick.

It starts when you drop a rope into a reed basket. The rope then rises out of the basket on its own in a straight line, shooting straight for the sky. If the trick goes as planned, the rope is so stiff and strong that a lanky, handsome person of Indian descent can ascend to the top and then descend safely. Upon the climber's return to the ground, the rope collapses. A true mystery.

Thanks to my scientific brain and your dedication to magic, this trick will now be part of your repertoire. The only downside is that you'll have to perform the illusion at the same place every time, so choose your location wisely.

Prep for this trick requires a shovel. Why? Because you have to dig. Actually, you'll be excavating so much earth that you'll want a friend or two to help. Ever heard of digging a hole to China? That's kind of what you're going to do. But your hole may not go to China. It may lead to Indonesia or some tiny unnamed island. Take a wrong turn, and you may find yourself in the middle of an ocean. Wherever it leads, dig a hole through Earth.

This feat accomplished, get a long metal pole to stretch through the entire planet. Earth's diameter is 7,917.5 miles, so you'll need a pole that long, with an extra 12 to 15 feet. Because the pole is this long, it should be made of something light and strong. Thanks to my unfettered access to an obscure technology known as the Internet, I learned of microlattice, a new metal created in 2015 by metal-making men and women. According to the pros, this stuff is as strong as titanium, while weighing hundreds of times less than Styrofoam. I recommend this material for your pole.

Once you dig the hole and secure a 7,917.5-mile-and-12-foot pole, you've got three more things to do.

**1.** Wrap the last 12 or 15 feet of the pole with rope and glue the rope in place.

**2.** Have a friend* on the other side of the planet hang out by the hole you dug.

**3.** Lower the pole through your side of the hole. Your friend (on the other side) should hold the pole so that it isn't visible above the basket.

Have those things done? Then it's time to get to the magic. Place your wicker basket over the hole you dug. (Note: Don't make the hole larger than the base of your basket. Having a basket fall through the Earth is a neat effect, but it's nowhere as cool as the Indian rope trick.) Now take an ordinary rope and let the audience feel it. Ideally, this rope will look similar to the rope you glued on the giant pole, but if it's close enough, it'll do. Amazement helps crowds forget details.

After convincing your audience that the rope is normal, toss it carefully (or carelessly—your choice) into the basket. Say a few magic words, and then act like you're mentally straining to force the magic words to do their job. (I think of geometry problems to give the impression of performing a difficult but meaningless task.) As you do mental math or recite poetry in your head, secretly text your friend to get to work.

As long as you've paid your phone bill and your friend's phone has good reception, the trick should be a hit from here. Upon receiving the text, your friend should begin pushing the pole into the ground from the other side of the world. When this happens, the pole will rise from the basket in front of you. When it reaches 12 feet, climb to the top and back down again before your admiring crowd. (Note: You may want to leave the climbing part to an assistant of Indian descent to avoid accusations of cultural appropriation, whether intentional or accidental.)

Upon landing, bang heartily on the pole. Once the vibrations reach the end of the pole, your friend will pull the pole her direction, causing it to disappear from your side. The crowd will gasp audibly. This is when you bow.

If you were careful with the placement of your regular rope, you can now pull it out of the basket to show that it has returned to its initial state. If you weren't careful with its placement, the rope may have fallen in and gotten incinerated by the Earth's core. Not a massive problem, but you'll have to buy another rope for the next performance.

Another quick note: Place a strong cover over your hole any time you're not performing. Leaving it open may cause minor legal issues, should a yapping poodle or teetering toddler fall through. The first time I set up this trick, my Great Aunt Matilda wandered into the hole and suffered a concussion. Her husband, my litigation-crazed Uncle Herbert, took me for all I was worth. Fortunately, I wasn't worth much at the time.

And a final note: The rope may not be the only thing to succumb to the Earth's core. Your pole may as well. However, that's a problem too extensive to be addressed in this small book. So you're on your own.

**There is a saying that encourages you to "Choose your friends wisely." This is never more important than when performing this illusion. Pick a friend lacking strength and you'll find yourself in dire straits. Actual dire straits. Not the band.*

# Standing Levitation

**Difficulty:** 5 out of 10
**Odds of Rocketing to an Unexpected Location:** 8 out of 10

Levitation has proven to be one of the most mysterious of magic skills. But take heart! Soon, you'll know how to take your levitation game to the next level and possibly even into the stratosphere.

Fancy footwork can give the illusion of levitation. With this technique, you'll actually levitate, possibly very high above the ground.

For this approach, you need a pair of propulsion machines. For the uninformed, the most common type of propulsion machine—and the type I recommend—is a jetpack. Unfortunately, you can't strap a gigantic jetpack on your back without being found out and torching the tails of your tux. So you'll need tiny jetpacks that strap to your ankles.

Velcro these smaller-than-average jetpacks to your ankles and sew the control module into your shirt sleeve. This enables you to discretely increase or reduce thrust as needed. With a robust understanding of how your mini-jetpacks function, you'll be less likely to shoot into orbit. So scan the owner's manual before liftoff. Once you feel confident in your knowledge, give the jetpacks a try.

After practicing with the mini-jetpacks for a while and learning where the jet flames shoot out, put on pants. I realize now that I should have told you to practice pantless. If you've already scorched your slacks, I apologize. But you won't do that again, will you? Proof positive that at times, experience truly is the best teacher.

Anyway, you've got pants on now. Hooray! Continue using the jets to propel yourself gently off the ground, only to descend again safely. Have it figured out? Good! Now do it for a crowd. Just be careful. One of the magician's worst enemies is adrenaline. While it's no big deal if adrenaline causes you to talk fast during a pick-a-card-any-card trick, it can be disastrous when dealing with jetpacks that are propelled by fire.

So relax. Remind yourself to push the throttle gently and focus on having a cool, calm, and collected liftoff. As you prepare to leave Mother Earth, consider the impression you want to leave on your audience. Modifying the impression is easy and can be done with each performance. For example, you may want to lift one or both fists in the air as a tip of the hat to Superman. Or maybe you want to hold your hands to your side, as if pushing yourself from the ground. Then again, maybe you want to crouch and leap into the air before you stay air-bound for an extended period. Any one of these is adequate and apropos. The choice depends on your personality and the crowd.

Do note that you'll need to cover up the sound of your jetpack. For this, keep

a troupe of breakdancers on staff. As you begin the illusion, these street-wise dancers should lay out their dance floor and slide a cassette in the tape deck. Immediately before your levitation begins, the dancers should hit the play button on the boom box. Use their loud, hip tunes as a cover, and do your trick at this moment. Just be careful when choosing dancers. They should be neither exceptionally skilled nor amazingly incompetent. Should they be either of these, your audience may shift focus onto the dancers rather than your levitation.

And a final note of caution. To prevent bystanders from having their clothing or epidermis charred, install a red velvet rope normally used to keep commoners from interacting with celebrities. If you're on a budget, police tape will do. With this rope (or tape) in place, you can perform without the fear of having to face an audience with singed mustaches and eyebrows. While burning off facial hair astounds audiences of all ages, leaving them in their non-scorched state leaves a more positive impression.

# Pudding Be Gone!

**Difficulty:** 1 out of 10
**Risk of Losing a Friend:** 8 out of 10

Ever spend your lunch period staring at the pudding snack stuffed in your best friend's pretentious lunch bag? Well, there's a remedy for that. You just need two skills.

**Skill 1:** An ability to consume an entire pudding cup in one slurp without choking and regurgitating the contents. Some crassly refer to this as "snarfing."

**Skill 2:** A willingness to ruin the friendship with your pudding-toting pal. Some say this isn't a skill, but those people aren't magicians. Magic is a lonely endeavor, and having everyone hate you ain't easy.

In addition to these skills, you need your friend's untouched pudding and a previous day's cup o' pudding. Yes, you have to plan for this one, but it's pretty easy. Just watch your friend toss a pudding cup in the trash and secretly retrieve it. Stuff it in your pants pocket for the next day, and wash it as soon as possible. Otherwise, the pudding will turn into liquid pudding residue that will dribble down your pant leg faster than you can say, "Abracadabra."

The following day, place the crushed, day-old pudding cup in your back pocket. When your volunteer* decides to get down to pudding-eating business, put an end to it. Tell your pal you'd like to do something impressive, but your friend can't eat that pudding just yet.

The friend will be intrigued and hopefully willing to hear you out. If not, your friend's a jerk. Get a new one. If he wants to see your impressive feat, ask for his pudding cup. He'll hesitate at first—not because it's his only pudding cup that day, but because it's his only pudding cup that day and he doesn't want to give it to you. And honestly, who can blame him?

Despite this hesitation, sweet talk your friend until he gives in. This is where it gets good.

Hold the pudding out in front of you. Lift it to the fluorescent lights that dangle from above. Look hard at the package, as if studying its content, making sure it's real pudding. Allow onlookers to join you in this viewing. Impress upon them the fact that there is real pudding in a real pudding container in your real hand. Everything is real, and this magic trick isn't a trick. It's reality.

Once everyone is convinced your pal's pudding is actual pudding, show the pudding one more time and nod. This little movement will signal that it's go time. It will also

put your viewers in the proper mindspace to receive the illusion.

Following your nod, whip the pudding behind your back and act as if you're ingesting it through your spine. Since there are no recorded incidents of someone eating pudding through the spine, you can be creative. No audience member will know what you should look like when eating pudding with your spine, so there's no wrong way to go about it.

As you pretend to shove pudding into the most delicate part of your body, back against the nearest cafeteria table. Gently set the pudding cup on it. Then remove the used, crinkled pudding package from your rear pocket and crumple and crush it behind your back for effect.

Before the looks of confusion, shock, and awe disappear from your viewers' faces, produce the used pudding container from behind your back, and toss it to your best friend. While everyone stares in awe at the smashed pudding cup, make a 180-degree turn so that your back is to the group. Quickly, but in a carefree manner, walk away with the full pudding cup in your hand. Rip the top off and down the pudding in one quick slurp. This ensures that when your best friend catches on to what happened and demands you give it back, he won't actually want it. Because it's yours now.

Should he be a real jerk about the whole thing, respond in kind and disperse the pudding lovingly into his hands for re-consumption.

**We call your friend a* volunteer, *because good magic always makes use of a volunteer. Besides, calling your friend a volunteer helps you feel better about the end result. Losing a volunteer hurts less.*

# Rabbit in the Hat

**Difficulty:** 1 out of 10 (unless you hate rabbits)
**Odds of Needing a Taxidermist Afterward:** 6 out of 10

This trick is so overdone that you may wonder why it's included in this edgy, state-of-the-art magic book. I include it because it's a classic, and no one will guess your technique. That's because no one has done it this way, despite the fact that every child suspects this is how the trick is performed.

There is, however, a prerequisite. You must be a master rabbit trainer. Okay, *master* may be overkill. You don't have to teach rabbits to dance or sing or memorize a long, drawn-out routine. You have to teach them to stay still—very still—even when tilted upside down while in a hat. Of course, this book can't go into the intricacies of training a rabbit to remain motionless for prolonged periods, but there are many excellent resources at your local library and pet store to get started.

With your trained bunny and top hat (the prerequisite for any serious magician), stuff the bunny inside the hat. As previously stated, make sure your bunny can lie very still and very flat. However, a squishy bunny isn't all you'll need. Audiences love it when a top hat is crumpled into a pancake-sized wafer. So make sure your hat can withstand such damage. Then sew a black flap of fabric inside the hat to cover the bunny until released from her hiding place.

Bunny in place, lay the fabric over her back. Fasten the fabric with Velcro. (I've used bubble gum for this task in the past. Although it kept the flap in place, the gum wound up in the rabbit's fur. The result was two hours of massaging peanut butter all over the little critter's back to remove the gum. The crowd grew restless and was rather confused when my bunny, which should have been a pure white rabbit, appeared to have climbed out of an extra crunchy jar of Skippy.) Once the rabbit stops squirming, put on your custom headgear and head to the stage. Show the crowd your hat, flipping it every which way. Smash it flat to convince the audience that it doesn't contain a hidden bunny. (Of course, your hat does contain a hidden bunny, but the audience doesn't know that. Oh, those poor, gullible onlookers!)

For the grand finale*, do what everyone expects you to do: pull the rabbit out of your hat. Not too fast, though! The furry thing has been plastered against your cranium to this point, so you'll need to prep the critter for public viewing.

Since this fluffing may take a while, gather a dozen or two rabbit-related jokes to keep your audience enthralled. Example:

**Q1.** How do you catch a unique rabbit?

**A1.** Unique up on it.

**Q2.** How do you catch a tame rabbit?

**A2.** The tame way.

With jokes like these, you're sure to delight your crowd. You may even keep them from storming the stage in outrage for taking so much time to finish the silly trick. And yes, it is silly. Because honestly, if you could perform real magic, would you be pulling small pets from hats? I'd guess you'd do something more impressive, such as ending world hunger or lowering rent prices in New York City. Anyway, make the jokes great. Because as you joke, you'll need to do the following:

**1.** Remove the black fabric covering your bunny's back. Do this by releasing the Velcro that holds it in place as quietly as possible.

**2.** Make sure your bunny is alive. This is pretty easy, even if you're untrained. Just place one finger on the tiny rabbit neck and feel for a bunny-sized pulse.

**3.** Using sleight of hand, produce a rabbit comb or brush, and comb or brush the bunny's fur. Otherwise, you'll yank a gross, matted, non-rabbit-looking creature from your top hat.

These three feats accomplished, you're ready for the final flourish. Gently lift the rabbit from the hat. I say gently, because that poor creature just spent the last ten to sixty minutes crammed in a flat compartment inside a hat, soaking in your scalp sweat. So as you can imagine, she won't be eager to please. Being gentle may be your only hope for producing a rabbit that won't gorge on your flesh for retribution.

Assuming the rabbit is in good spirits, hold the creature high, allowing the crowd to see and adore her. Give the bunny a treat, and then send her on an all-expenses-paid

spa weekend with her bunny buddies. She deserves it.

A quick note here: If your rabbit becomes lifeless at any point, stop the trick and move to the next one. To transition seamlessly, fling the hat with the bunny still inside to the back of the stage, comment that the "Bunny doesn't want to come out and play today after all—because she's dead," and keep going. Most audience members will think you're joking and will enjoy what they presume is yet another trick.

**There is actually no extra information included here. I expected some readers had grown accustomed to these asterisked remarks, so I felt obliged to leave one for their enjoyment. Do note, however, that some future illusions offer no asterisks. Please don't be alarmed.*

# Vanishing Man

**Difficulty:** 20 out of 10
**Odds of Performing This Trick:** 0 out of 10

Everyone dreams of making someone disappear. Whether an annoying little brother, a coworker, or the gal who's going twenty in a forty-five mile-per-hour zone, getting rid of someone on the quick would make your life more enjoyable. Granted, if you cause the lady driving in front of you to vanish, things could get hairy, but some risks are worth taking.

Until now, there's not been a legal method to cause a person to disappear from planet Earth. This trick allows you to make someone go bye-bye without being convicted by the criminal justice system. Or at least you'll leave behind no evidence.

Here's how.

Before starting, you need someone willing to be disappeared. Finding this person in normal, everyday life is difficult. Fortunately, magic shows are overflowing with eager volunteers. These folks foolishly believe you're going to make them disappear for a moment, only to reappear at the rear of the auditorium wearing a janitor's outfit and speaking with a British accent.

Well, this one goes a bit further. You're going to make someone disappear, never to be seen again. At least not during the show. If there's something magic audiences love, it's mystery, and this trick is nothing but mystery! Once a volunteer is picked, it's time for small talk. Get his name, favorite color, and any other information you desire. Honestly, this information won't be used for any magical purpose. All this does is verify your suspicion that the individual before you could do with a good vanishing. So ask questions to gain peace of mind about causing your volunteer to disappear, and patiently store up your magical wrath.

Next, perform flourishes that will prime the audience for the most amazing trick ever displayed. As they pant and scream in anticipation, finish the trick with whatever effect you desire. By *effect*, I mean you can make it look extremely difficult or supremely simple. It doesn't matter. Make the person disappear, and no one will care how challenging it appears.

Now to get to the meat of the trick, the how-do-you-make-the-person-disappear part. After the bravado and build-up, how do you actually make a person disappear? Especially since there are to be no curtains, smoke machines, or mirrors?

To be frank, I've not worked out all the details just yet.* But it will be pretty sweet once I do. I may even write a standalone book to explain how to do it. It'll be that good.**

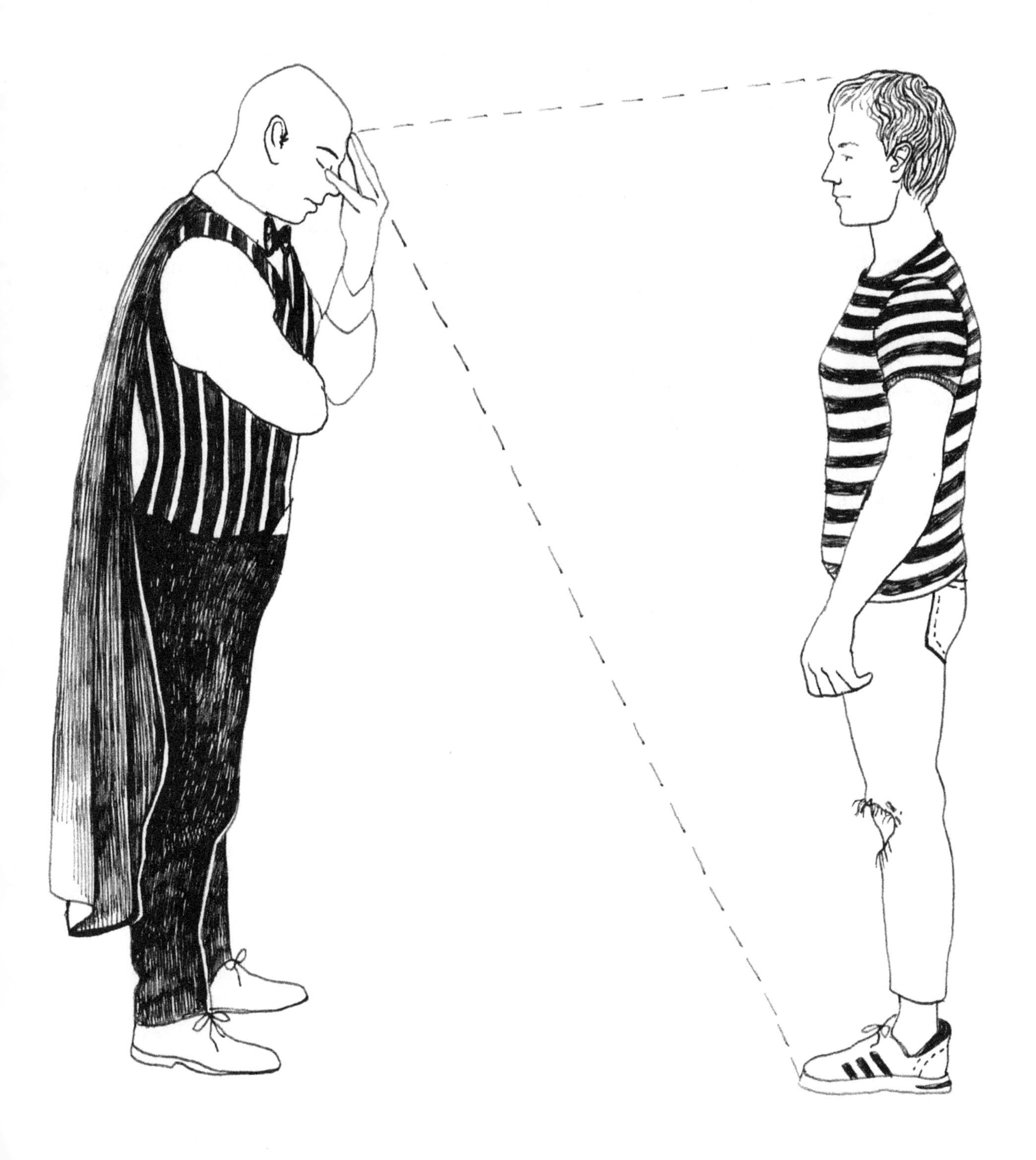

In the meantime, if there are any aspiring magicians who figure out just how to make someone disappear without using a weapon or trapdoor, please email your method to the staff of Sir Brody Books at sirbrodybooks@gmail.com. I will use your information to write the aforementioned book. While you will not reap any financial reward (leave that burden to me), you will be credited as my research assistant. This will offer the attention that you, like all magicians, so desperately crave.

**How does a world-renowned magic-book author find himself in such an embarrassing predicament? My publisher demanded I include this trick and pressured me into publishing an innovative methodology, despite the fact that I've not yet determined one. I caved to this demand, proving my chiropractor's suspicion that I am indeed spineless.*

***I can only assume it will be good enough for a standalone book, as my publisher so adamantly forced the issue.*

# Bullet Catch

**Difficulty:** 9.4 out of 10
**Likelihood You'll Die Tryin':** 8 out of 10

Through the years, a handful of illusionists have performed the bullet catch. Most notable is Coulen of Lorraine, the earliest recorded performer of the trick. Sadly, Coulen's assistant bludgeoned him with the butt of the gun used in the trick. But not even Coulen—if he were alive—could uncover the secret to this new technique, because it's fresh, inventive, unexpected, and genuinely magical.

Ready to make heads spin by catching a bullet with your teeth? Keep reading.

While the bullet catch is frequently performed by duos, this methodology frees you from needing a partner who's in on the act. More important than a partner is a piece of equipment that can be found on eBay or Craigslist. That piece of equipment? A mech-

anism that pauses time, often referred to as a "time pauser."

In the event you can't find a pausing machine, a regular time machine will suffice. But make sure it's precise. Disappear in the middle of your trick only to wind up ten years in the future at another location, and your audience would leave very confused. To make matters worse, it would likely result in the second-degree murder of any stagehand in the line of fire. Potentially worse still, time would never start again, resulting in a major malfunction in the space-time continuum, an event that would send Emmett "Doc" Brown into panic mode.

But let's not get ahead of ourselves. After all, I'm not dealing with rookie magicians. You know where to buy a functional time-pausing machine. Now I'll explain how to use it to your illusional advantage.

Show your gun of choice to the audience. A revolver is a good option. There's something visceral, nostalgic, and dangerous about them. After letting an audience member or two handle the gun, load a few rounds and shoot at a target. Ensure the target is placed in such a way as to not put your audience at risk. Remember: the trick involves you catching a bullet with your teeth, not an audience member catching one in the gut.

As the smoke wisps away from the end of your gun barrel, the audience should realize that you're using a real gun with real bullets. And that's good, because you are. To make it more obvious that you're not firing blank rounds, use a target that will explode, like a two-liter bottle of generic soda. Shooting name-brand soda costs more upfront and may offend potential sponsors, costing you even more in the long run. Of course, if you're trying to land generic soda sponsors, shoot at name-brand sodas. Then again, since soda wreaks havoc on your teeth's enamel, repairing soda-damaged teeth may cost more than any sponsorship will pay.

From this point, hand a round of ammunition to an audience member. Have the volunteer sign or otherwise mark the tip of the bullet. I recommend full metal-jacket ammo, as hollow-point bullets expand on impact. Cool as an expanded bullet looks, the expansion will deform the signature and cast doubt upon your illusion.

With the ammunition signed, allow the volunteer to insert the cartridge into the firearm. If he's not gun savvy, load the round into the chamber yourself. If you're not gun savvy, get another volunteer or drop the illusion from your routine. Having two gun-un-savvy people load a weapon in a room full of people is a recipe for disaster.

Gun loaded, pause reality or put your time machine into effect. Again, it's best if you simply pause time. So with that in mind, the rest of the trick will be explained, assuming you can stop time without the cumbersome demands a time machine places upon you. With time paused, slide the weapon out of the volunteer's hand. Shoot the weapon into a surface that will stop the bullet without ricocheting.* A half dozen phone books should do the trick. Fire into the phone books, retrieve the bullet, and place a blank round in the weapon. Reinstall the weapon in your volunteer's hand, place the signed and shot bullet between your teeth, get into position, and restart time.

Your volunteer will pull the trigger, and you'll pretend to catch the bullet between your teeth. Validate the illusion by spreading your lips to show the bullet between them. For the grand finale, have your volunteer remove the bullet and confirm that it's the same bullet that he marked prior to the trick.

Take a bow, and wipe the sweat from your brow. Because had you not stopped time at the right moment, your family would be submitting a rush order for your tombstone.

And as has been proven time and again, no one likes magic tricks that end in death.

On further consideration, a revolver may not be best. With a semi-automatic pistol, you can turn on the gun's safety, a mechanism not found on revolvers. Should you opt for a pistol, you're more intelligent than I imagined. Upon replacing the real round with a blank one, turn off the safety, and you may restart time with minimal risk to your person. Assuming your audience members aren't sticklers for detail, no one will notice that the safety was tampered with mid-performance.

**Lesser magicians have neglected to consider ricochet. When you have a free weekend, we can visit their graves.*

# Bullet Catch (Low-Tech Technique)

**Difficulty:** 36 out of 10
**Likelihood You'll Die Tryin':** Yes

Don't want to invest in a time-pausing machine? No sweat. With a little dedication, you can still have a stellar illusion. However, if you don't have the reflexes of a jaguar, you'll need to practice an inordinate amount of time before attempting this approach.

Begin training by instructing a child to throw a tennis ball at your face. As long as you don't get hit in the eye too often, you can practice for hours on end. The goal is to grab the ball before it smacks you in the face. Do this over and over to build muscle memory.

Once you can catch the ball at least two out of five times without getting hit in the snout, move to something a bit more dangerous. I suggest a stone. Preferably one that is the size of a baseball. That way, you can get used to catching something hard. As you become more proficient at catching the stone with your hand (and not your grill), chip away at it with a small hammer until it is the size of a bullet.

The smaller the stone gets, the harder it is to throw. At some point in your training, your assistant should begin using a slingshot. Whether shooting small stones, marbles, or nuts and bolts at your kisser, a slingshot in the hands of a moderately able individual can hit the same location with great consistency at great speeds. Ideally, your slingshot shooter will send whatever object you're using sailing toward your pouty lips over and over and over. (Note: One bad shot requires days of rehabilitation, but without access to a time-pausing mechanism, this is your only option.)

Now, to catch the object with your teeth. If you're not ready to catch a marble or small rock with your teeth on day one, take it slowly. Instead of attempting to catch the marble or bullet-sized rock, let it graze off your teeth and continue moving past you. Practice seeing the object moving at a high speed and learn to follow it with your face. Do this long enough, and you'll learn how to make even the smallest item scrape your teeth in passing. When you feel confident with this skill, try to catch the flying item with your teeth.

Upon being able to catch pebbles slung from a slingshot, flaming arrows from any distance, and grapes tossed at you from across the room, you're ready to catch a bullet with your teeth. Stand at the ready, and tell your assistant to shoot directly at your face on the count of three. Count to three, and catch the bullet.

The payoff of this bullet catch is identical to the previous version: part your lips and show the bullet between your teeth. Allow the assistant to remove the bullet and verify it has the same markings placed there earlier. Finally, take a bow.

For interested professionals, there is a more dramatic ending following a successful catch. (An alternate ending also exists if your catch doesn't go well, but we won't discuss that here.) Assuming you've strengthened your teeth with fluoride and improved your coordination beyond comprehension, you're prepared for an amazing illusion conclusion. Once the bullet is confirmed as the proper one, take it from your assistant and pop it in your mouth. It's normal for the crowd to gasp. After all, you already caught a moving bullet with your teeth. What more could you do?

With a wink of the eye, begin chewing. Bullets are made of lead, a soft metal that—for those with well-enameled teeth—can be broken easily into small pieces. Orally break the bullet into 30 or 40 well-formed BBs.

With these in your cheeks, motion for your assistant to bring out a turkey choke. Used to increase the range and accuracy of shotguns while hunting turkey, a turkey choke normally screws into a shotgun barrel. For this illusion, you'll not use a shotgun. Instead, place the choke in your mouth like an athletic whistle and position the mouth-made BBs into a tight wad at the front of your mouth, directly against the backside of the choke.

Have your assistant release a wild turkey from backstage. (For the uninitiated, it's commonplace in the magic world to have a caged wild turkey backstage at every show.) The bird will trot into the audience's view from the opposite side of the stage. As soon as you have a good shot, spew the BBs as a single unit toward the bird. With any luck, you'll place half a dozen shots in the fowl's neck. Thus assaulted, the turkey will keel over instantly.

Admittedly, this is a shocking display of power that has varying effects on different

individuals. Some will screech in horror. Others will stand in awe. Even others may vomit or call the police. But all is not lost. You can bring the crowd back to their senses with the smell of your kill being slow-cooked over an open fire. In fact, by the time you complete your show and the bird is served, the audience will be eating from your hand. Literally. Unless having people eat turkey from your hand is off-putting for you. Then they can serve themselves, but you'll have to pass out plates, forks, and napkins—a process I find excessively time consuming and unnecessarily expensive. Besides, having people eat out of your hand makes for powerful newspaper headlines.

A note about this special ending: Though it can be gratifying to take down a full-grown tom with a single bullet, it's much more difficult to do so. So don't be tempted to leave your bullet unchewed. Besides, it's illegal in many states to hunt turkey with anything except shotgun shells. So chewing the bullet into small BBs gives you an air of authenticity and legality. Also, should your shot miss, a single bullet from a 9mm or .357 would put a rather large hole in whatever is behind the turkey. Smaller BBs, on the other hand, will lose velocity faster and cause less damage to walls and turkey meat.

Please note that this tremendous, terrifying trick has one overlooked health hazard. Because you're using your pearly whites to catch flying objects, your enamel may wear off. Guard against this by requesting fluoride treatment from your dentist every six months. Yes, it tastes disgusting and makes your teeth feel weird afterward. But there's no better way to keep enamel from chipping. So be a smart magician, and go for the full fluoride every six months.

# Peanut Butter Pie

**Difficulty:** 2 out of 10
**Odds of Regaining Previously Lost Friend(s):** 7 out of 10 (would be higher, were it not for rampant peanut allergies)

While other tricks are meant to overwhelm or gross out viewers, this one has a more innocent end goal: delight. To knock this one out, you'll need some very common tricks of the trade.

So head into your parents' kitchen and grab 1/2 a cup of peanut butter. While you're there, you may as well snag a 9-inch graham cracker crust, 4 ounces of softened cream cheese, 3/4 cup of confectioner's sugar, 1/2 a cup of milk, and 8 ounces of thawed, whipped topping.

With these ingredients, use a wizard's combining wand (commonly referred to as a whisk) to combine the cream cheese and confectioner's sugar. Then mix in the peanut butter and milk, beating them together until you have a smooth mixture. Fold in the whipped topping, and toss it onto the crust.

This is where the magic takes a turn for the boring. Put your creation in the freezer, and walk away. The next few hours are dull. So dull that some magicians pull this trick from their act. If you have three hours of other magic material, lead your set with this trick and finish with it three hours later. You can try your hand at jokes, but unless you're really funny, two or three hours of magic-related punch lines are hard to stomach.

Anyway, once that thing's been in the freezer for three hours, pull it out. To continue amazing people, eat the entire thing in one sitting. Doing that without going into a sugar coma or blowing chunks one direction or another is impressive. More impressive, however, is using this illusion to help your audience find a state of happiness.

This is achieved with a simple technique. Take a knife (you'll want a sharp one, since you're cutting through frozen peanut butter) and slice the creation into wedges. Take the individual pieces, set them on paper plates, and distribute them to the audience. Hand out plastic forks, and watch happiness take over.

To guarantee success, perform this trick before an audience of individuals you've wronged. Think of the person whose pudding you sucked down in an instant (see "Pudding Be Gone!" on page 43) or maybe the person you sawed in half ("Sawing Someone in Half," page 13). Not only will this pie make that person happy, but you may regain your friendship. Not having a rough go with any relationships? Use this one to impress that special someone. It'll work every time!

Note: Astute magicians will claim this trick is no illusion, but is basic cooking for

the unskilled, culinary rookie. In response, I would have you know that cooking is magic. You take a bunch of random stuff, toss it together, and it tastes magically delicious. On top of that, you can put smiles on people's faces. Just make sure, if this is a make-up pie—I mean illusion—do not accidentally dump laxatives in the mixture. That will not help the problem. In truth, doing that may cause an otherwise healthy relationship to blow up and splatter against the wall.

# Cups and Balls

**Difficulty:** 4 out of 10
**Odds You'll Butcher This Ancient Classic:** 7 out of 10

Remember the beginning of this book, when I mentioned a guy named Dedi? He's the first person recorded to do a magic trick, and that trick was the disappearing balls trick, also known as cups and balls. Granted, some of that information is disputed. But, hey, we're all professionals here. So put away your "David-Copperfield-is-the-first-and-best-magician-ever" statements and assume cups and balls was indeed done more than 4,500 hundred years ago.

Now that we've got that out of the way, let's move ahead.

The trick is easy. You just have to know what you're doing. All you need (in case you've not studied this trick to death in the past) are a table, three cups, and three balls.

For cups, I use those plastic ones that come with kids' meals at fancy restaurants.* The balls should be the size of a Ping-Pong ball, but without the bounce. Unless you're cocky. Then, use balls that bounce to the moon.

Anyway, to start the trick, show the audience that there's nothing inside the cups. Then slowly and deliberately set each cup upside down on the table.

Produce the balls and place all three on top of a single cup.** Many magicians place all three balls on the far-right cup. That's fine. But you can place them on any cup. Granted, there are only three cups, so you don't have many options. But some people don't have even three cups from which to choose, so if you do, count yourself fortunate.

Once the trio of balls is safely atop your cup of choice, the magic begins. Take the three balls into your hand (yes, pick up the balls you set down just moments earlier) and count them in front of the crowd. If the trick has gone well thus far, there won't be three balls in your hand. Rather, there will be two. With a surprised look on your face, lift the cup on which the balls were previously resting. The crowd will be delighted to see the third ball made its way under the cup.

Impressive, but there's more. Place the cup back over the ball. Lift the other two cups to show there's no ball under either. The next time you raise the first cup, the ball will be missing.

The crowd will gasp, and weaker individuals may run from the theater screaming. That's both expected and accepted. Most people aren't accustomed to being in front of a real-life magician. But the surprises don't end there.

Lift the second cup, which recently had nothing under it. There will be a ball there. Still holding the second cup with one hand, use your free hand to lift the third cup. The

other two balls are now under the third cup.

Yes, this is surprising, but hold on tight, 'cause we've only just begun!

Pick up all three balls from under the two cups, and slide the balls into your jacket pocket. Set the cups back on the table. Lift the first cup. Magically, all three balls will have made their way under it. Grab the balls, set the cup back down, and then quickly lift all three cups, one at a time. To both your surprise and that of the audience, a single ball will be under each cup, none in your pocket, and none in your hands.

How does this work? It's magic. And if you're a magician, the balls will go where they ought. If you're not a magician, take up a new craft, such as sewing, driving a bulldozer, or writing fictitious how-to books.

Assuming you are a magician, continue lifting cups as many times and in any order you desire. The balls will jump from one cup to another and will even wind up on top of the cups or in audience members' clothing. I'm not sure how the balls jump out and about, but it happens. Trust me. I've seen lots of magicians do it.

The trick goes on like this until something happens that will amaze the audience and even you. The amazing something is that the balls will turn into something else. They may become larger balls. Or some pieces of fruit. Then again, you may wind up with a duckling under one or more of your cups, a small brick, a computer mouse, a tiny capybara, or a pile of watch batteries.

Once these unexpected objects appear, end the trick. My understanding is that if you continue, goblins will pop out from under the cups and consume you on the spot. While a powerful finale, being eaten alive prevents you from repeating the trick. Stop, and the items that materialized under your cups will return to their original ball shapes following eight hours of rest, assuming you don't expose them to sunlight or water.

**The cups you choose can be any color. Should you feel particularly bold, you can go with clear cups. One famous duo uses clear plastic cups, and the trick goes off without a hitch every single time. I'd guess that if they can do it, you can, too!*

***If you can't fit all three balls on top of a single cup bottom, fetch smaller balls or get some bigger cups.*

# Magic Coloring Book

**Difficulty:** 7 out of 10
**Risk of Ruining a Coloring Book:** Is this a real concern?

A regular at children's birthday parties, this illusion isn't easy, even when using the traditional technique. To perform it in a mind-blowing manner, which you're about to learn, you must master sleight of hand and possess superb hand-third-eye coordination.

Ready to blow some minds?

Grab a coloring book and head to the stage. Display the contents of the coloring book and explain that it's a magic coloring book. Show the audience the inside of the coloring book, which only contains uncolored drawings. Then pace the stage, holding the coloring book behind you.

As you walk back and forth, tell your audience a story about the coloring book. People like the idea that a coloring book has a (pardon the pun) colorful past. Whether it came from an ancient coloring master in the Middle East or you found it beside a drainage ditch inside a pizza box doesn't matter. What does matter is that your story captivates the audience long enough for you to color each page.

As you stroll and tell your story, use the crayons hidden in your sleeves to color the drawings inside the book. For the newbie, this can take as long as thirty minutes, so you'll need a really good story to keep your audience engaged.

At some point in your tale, mention that magic coloring books are often visited by coloring fairies. When this happens, the book is magically colored in a matter of seconds. Explain that at this very moment, a coloring fairy could be sneaking inside your coloring book and going crazy, coloring every drawing in the entire book. Give sufficient detail to buy the time necessary to color each picture.

Coloring complete, tuck the crayons back inside your sleeve. Take a deep breath, and open the book to show that your coloring book has somehow become colored.

Struggle to color inside the lines? You're not the first. Save your act by telling the audience that coloring fairies are erratic and messy with their art. It's just how they are. The crowd will believe you and clap appreciatively, because that's what audiences do. As they do this, you'll stand tall, proud that you pulled the wool over the eyes of another crowd of sheep. But you should know that the illusion isn't complete just yet. You've got to return the book to its original state. And as with most magic tricks, this is easier said than done.

The best technique is to repeat the same actions performed when coloring the

book, but this time with Wite-Out. The only downside is that your audience won't want to wait another thirty minutes, even if you're a great storyteller. So make it fast!

The coloring book now Wited-Out, it's ready to be shown to your audience. Since you probably got Wite-Out all over everything, including the line drawings, the pages will be blanker than when you first began. This makes the illusion even more impressive.

All that's left is to bow and blow kisses to the crowd. Do this with gusto and bathe in the crowd's love.

To perform this trick again, purchase another coloring book at your local coloring book retailer and scrub the Wite-Out from your hands and shirtsleeves.

# Self-Healing Rope

**Difficulty:** 2 out of 10
**Extra Benefit:** Future paper cuts will heal faster

Excited about learning this trick? Good for you. Skip the next few sentences and pick up on the paragraph that starts with the word *Rope.*

Now, a note for magicians who think this trick is wimpy: I agree. Adding this trick wasn't my idea. My grandmother told me that some people are afraid of stainless steel blades and others don't have the wherewithal to dig a hole from one side of the globe to the next. I told Grandma that I'm not writing this book for those people. However, she pointed out that tossing a bone to the weak and weak-kneed will boost my sales. I considered her comment and decided to slip this puny trick into my otherwise impressive book. But don't worry! I didn't add it in as a marketing ploy. I refuse to sell out to make a quick buck. Rather, I included this silly trick out of love for Grandma. Also, if you know a weak or weak-kneed "magician," don't tell said "magician" what's in this paragraph. No reason to unnecessarily offend. Especially since such a "magician" (notice that I repeatedly wrote the word *magician* in quotation marks as an insult) probably suffers from low self-esteem.

Rope is good.

Okay, now that everyone is back with us, let's discuss how to do this trick in a mind-blowing way. It starts with what my mother called "Magic Medicine." I find this name particularly apropos, as this is a "magic" book. For those who grew up outside of my home on Timberlane Trail, Magic Medicine is triple antibiotic ointment. A very common name-brand version of the stuff sells widely, but mentioning it by name would cost half a million bucks. (Hint: It starts with *Neo* and ends with *sporin*.)

Anyway, you'll need some Magic Medicine. But before you start squirting the healing ointment into your palm, grab a piece of rope. It doesn't have to be super long, super strong, super thick, or full of shtick. Just get a piece, and make sure it doesn't fall apart in your hands.

Now that you have your Magic Medicine and rope, combine the two. While you could mix them in a bowl with an electric beater, I recommend applying Magic Medicine to the rope by hand. Put it on thick, like the rope has a festering wound from fourth grade that still hasn't healed. Unless your rope is in third grade. Then apply it as if the rope has been wounded since kindergarten.

With the rope well-lubed, toss it in a plastic container, and wash your hands. For seven days, do as you wish. Carve a black bear from a solid piece of wood, earn your doctorate online, or become a real magician and dig a hole to the other side of planet Earth.

During these seven days, your rope will absorb the Magic Medicine. At the end of the absorption period, the rope shouldn't be too greasy to the touch. To the casual observer, the rope will be a random rope carried around by a random magician. But this rope is anything but ordinary. It's superordinary!

If you don't get a decent booking to show off your illusion, book it to the nearest street corner where people can safely stop to watch your illusion.

Once there, gather a good crowd. Otherwise, what's the point of magic? With a crowd of two hundred or half a dozen, pull out your doctored rope. Let one lucky audience member feel the rope, pull on it, chew it—whatever convinces him that it's a normal rope.

Now, take the rope. Double it over and whip out a cutting instrument. You can use safety scissors, but they don't exude danger or cool. And with this trick, you need all the made-up excitement you can muster. So use something more dangerous and manly. Example: a Bowie knife. Should you choose this particular cutting edge, you may also put on your red shoes and dance the blues.

Whatever cutting instrument you decide upon, cut the rope. Double the two pieces over and over again. Do it a third time for good measure. Then cut the rope another time or two. You now hold between 16 and 1,000 pieces of rope. Grasp the rope pieces in such a way that both ends of each piece are visible.

With all these pieces dangling from your hand, promise a miracle. Tell the crowd that you're going to join the pieces of rope back together, without a single knot. Don't be surprised when viewers express doubt and even walk out on you. Don't be disappointed either. You don't need them.

Have one of the remaining onlookers join you at center sidewalk. Keep one piece of rope and give all other pieces to your new assistant. Confirm that you don't know each other. Then compliment your assistant's outfit if she's a female. Women like that kind of stuff, and it helps the crowd know you're a great person. If a male is chosen, say something sarcastic, such as "You smell funny." This will elicit laughs and put your assistant at ease, as men thrive on insults.

Once the warm fuzzy feelings pass or the laughter dies down, have your volunteer hand you a piece of rope. If things go well, he'll obey. Take the rope, and firmly press its end to the end of the rope you were already holding. Furrow your brow. According to Leonard Spink's *How to Look and Act Like a Magician*, this expression indicates deep concentration. After twenty or thirty seconds, the two pieces should stick together. This isn't because of any sticky substance. It's because the Magic Medicine you applied has worked to heal the injured rope. While it takes a week for Magic Medicine to heal a small scrape or cut, the healing time is reduced when dealing with inanimate objects.

From this point, continue connecting cut pieces to the ever-growing rope in your hands. When finished, wipe your hands on your pants to remove the shimmer of Magic Medicine, wave your free hand in the air, and toss the rope to viewers who want to verify the miracle that took place before their very eyes.

# Sticking Headphones

**Difficulty:** 3 out of 10
**Meanness:** 7.8 out of 10

Sometimes, magic tricks are more trick than magic. This is one of those times. Don't imagine this means that this illusion is easy though. Even the most humble effect requires precision and timing to achieve the desired outcome.

Before launching into the sticking headphones trick, shove a tube of superglue up your shirtsleeve and mount a pair of headphones on your magical head. Make sure a friend is sitting nearby, but not too close. Wait for that pal to have something to tell you. It doesn't matter what she has to say. It may be extremely important or extremely unimportant.

**Example #1 of something important:** Your nose is bleeding and staining your new white tennis shoes.

**Example #1 of something unimportant:** Your mom makes really good lasagna.

**Example #2 of something important:** Magic helps us see the world with awe and wonder and delight.

**Example #2 of something unimportant:** Magic is awesome, and you can't do it.

Now that you have a feel for the comments that may come your way, prepare for what's next. When your listening is interrupted, slowly pry the headphones from your skull, acting as if they're stuck there. Since you're a magician, feigning such things should be a breeze.

Once you get the headphones off your head, slump over dramatically to indicate that you're exhausted from the effort. Put on a solid performance and the person who bothered you will likely show concern for your health and well-being. When she asks if you're okay, shrug and turn away as if you're in too much residual pain to answer.

Now comes the tricky part. Place the headphones in your lap and drop the tube of superglue into your palm. (I forgot to mention this earlier, but you should pre-puncture the tube and stick it up your sleeve. Just be sure to replace the lid or you'll wind up with a tube of superglue attached to your arm.) Using sleight-of-hand skills (see other magic books to learn this skill), quickly and deftly spread glue around the fat, soft part of the headphones. Recap the tube, and slide it back up your shirtsleeve.

By now, the person who interrupted your headphone enjoyment will be curious. So curious that she'll come over and pat you gently on the shoulder.

"You okay?" she'll ask.

"Yeah," you'll say, "I guess so. It's just that…"

Here, hold for a long, dramatic pause. Make the caring person prod you to continue. Then sigh and give in.

"This pair of headphones is just so frustrating."

At this, the person you're speaking with may display a blank look. That indicates that you've got the perfect person for this illusion.

Continue by saying, "I put the headphones on and they sound great—better than most, actually. The only problem is that after leaving them on for five or ten minutes, they're almost impossible to get off!"

Note: While holding the headphones in your lap, keep them from touching each other. Otherwise, the trick is a no-go, because the headphones will be inseparable.

"Impossible to get off?" she'll ask, laughing at the thought. "You're kidding, right?"

Insist that you're not kidding. Say something about a voodoo princess doing what voodoo princesses do—that she put a hex on your headphones. And any time you listen to rock-and-roll for a long time, the headphones get harder to remove. Say the voodoo lady promised that the headphones would eventually stick to your head forever.

Hopefully, your friend won't believe you. Full of confidence, she'll want to check out the cursed headphones. So hand them to your soon-to-be-former pal. Or better yet, place the headphones on her ears. Remind her that the magic happens after five or ten minutes, so relax and enjoy the music. Then hit play on your MP3 player, and walk away. Far, far away.

Within a few minutes, the novelty of hexed headphones will wear off, and your friend will decide to test the curse. By now, you should be so far away that you can avoid being hit with whatever objects your friend lobs your way.

From a distance, encourage your former friend to seek out warm, soapy water in which to soak the headphones. This should eventually loosen the bond of the glue, allowing your former friend to remove the headphones.

If this doesn't help, acetone-based fingernail polish remover may do the trick. Of course, to supply this information to the unknowing volunteer, you'll have to get close enough to be heard.

This is where a trustworthy assistant comes in handy. Send the assistant with a box of chocolates or an envelope of money as a please-forgive-me token, and have your assistant help the poor sap.

For maximum likelihood of being forgiven, videotape the illusion. Tell your friend the video will be on YouTube and is sure to become a viral sensation. Because nothing cheers up someone like the promise of temporary Internet fame.

# Magician's Glossary

**Apropos**—If you know what the word *appropriate* means, you know what *apropos* means. It just sounds cooler. Tip: Don't enunciate the *s* at the end of the word. It would not be suitable.

**Asphalt**—The black stuff on the road that you drive on. One company that produces asphalt says its product allows yuppies to ride four wheelers.

**Catalytic converter**—What a muffler expert told me I needed to replace on a truck I purchased from my brother-in-law. Since the vehicle was already ten years old, I opted to see how long the truck could drive without spending another six hundred dollars for a part I didn't want. So far, so good! As an aside, *catalytic converter* was in the original manuscript of *The Only Magic Book You'll Never Need*. Though it was edited out, I left it here as a free bonus. You're welcome.

**Cultural Appropriation**—Participating in or enjoying activities, styles, or goods that don't originate from your native culture. Examples include Scandinavians speaking Italian, Nigerians wearing kilts, Koreans eating tacos, and Americans being content.

**Deftly**—Contrary to what your ears hear, this word has nothing to do with hearing. It means "with great skill and precision" or something along those lines. Of course, I'm sure that some people are deftly skilled at hearing.

**Dinghy**—A small boat with an embarrassing name. Because it's such a small boat, these are traditionally well kempt, unlike anything dingy.

**Disconcerting**—The opposite of concerting.

**Exhaustive**—Something that goes on and on until there is no more going on that can occur. Example: the talk your parents will give you after learning you read this book.

**Elicit**—Kind of like solicit, only no one posts signs against it.

**Feign**—A fancy way to say "fake." It's pronounced like the last name of David Blaine, who claims no relation to the word.

**Hexed**—It's kind of like being bamboozled, which can cause you to feel discombobulated. When someone is hexed, it is because of a spell. Not a short-time kind of spell or a spelling bee, but the type of spell Hermione was praised for mastering.

**Inordinate**—Not ordinate.

**Intricacies**—Small details that are often found in doilies, brooches, and adult coloring books.

**Juncture**—A word that was beloved by a former president during a specific time or place.

**Laxative**—Medication meant to help an individual with difficulty having a bowel movement. When given to an individual with regular bowel function, the results are messy. I do not recommend adding this to brownies, cookies, or cakes that you plan to share with friends.

**Prerequisite**—Something you've got to have before doing something else. To be a magician, one prerequisite is the willingness to lead a lonely life.

**Propulsion**—The action of pushing something forward. Sounds boring until you realize propulsion made it possible for you to be born.

**Purveyor**—A dude who purveys (a.k.a. sells) stuff to you at the right (or wrong) price.

**Skeptic**—Also known as nonbelievers, skeptics get called lots of things in magic circles: jerks, morons, stupid heads, and other harsh names that really bother them.

**Stratosphere**—A word that some bookish people say was misused in this delightful how-to manual. I would like to remind those individuals that this is a magic book, not a commentary on the proper use of language.

**Suffice**—To be enough or adequate. Example: If this is the only book you have on hand to learn magic, it will suffice.

**Wherewithal**—Something you need to be a big-time magician. If you don't know what it is, you're in trouble.

# About the Author

D.K. Brantley is an aging, musclebound husband and father. He recently wrote a magic book, which was a mistake, considering he can't palm a card and has never performed Houdini's milk can escape.

# About the Illustrator

Ekaterina Khozatskaya loves all things capybara and speaks in a movie-villain accent. As is customary for female magicians, she wears heels when waving a magic wand overhead.

# Other Titles Available By Sir Brody Books

**The Long Goodbye: journey to a miracle**

*By Sara Jane Briggs*

By the time Larry Briggs was diagnosed with a rare disease, he had less than six months to live. This book chronicles the struggles and fears that his wife, Sara Jane, experienced as Larry's disease progressed, and the miraculous, world-altering healing God performed on Larry.

**I'm 12 Years Old And I Saved The World**

*By D.K. Brantley*

I'm Adam—Adam Shannon Dakota Carr. Yeah, it's a terrible name. But it gets worse. I've got a super lame cell phone, and Mom won't let me cut my hair. As if things aren't bad enough, Dad lost his job and Mom and Dad's marriage is on the rocks. Now it's up to me to fix everything. That's right—I'm 12 years old, and I'm about to save the world.

**I'm 13 Years Old And I Changed The World**

*By D.K. Brantley*

Mom still won't let me cut my hair. I still share a bedroom with Grandpa. And my cell phone is still stuck in the Stone Age. But I've got a serious problem now. Big Mike has cancer, and I've got to step in and do what science hasn't yet done. I've got to find a cure. That's right—I'm 13 years old, and I'm about to change the world.

# LOVE IT?
# HATE IT?
# REVIEW IT!

Sir Brody Books and other independent book publishers live and die on fine folks like you spreading the word.

So leave a review online.

You'll make us feel special, and you may help someone else find a new favorite book in the process.

CPSIA information can be obtained
at www.ICGtesting.com
Printed in the USA
BVHW080706020420
576569BV00002B/89